Law of Transgender Rights in India

A Practical Guide for Transgenders

Dr Binoy Gupta

Ukiyoto Publishing

All global publishing rights are held by

Ukiyoto Publishing

Published in 2023

Content Copyright © Dr Binoy Gupta

ISBN 9789360161125

All rights reserved.
No part of this publication may be reproduced, transmitted, or stored in a retrieval system, in any form by any means, electronic, mechanical, photocopying, recording or otherwise, without the prior permission of the publisher.

The moral rights of the author have been asserted.

This is a work of fiction. Names, characters, businesses, places, events, locales, and incidents are either the products of the author's imagination or used in a fictitious manner. Any resemblance to actual persons, living or dead, or actual events is purely coincidental.

This book is sold subject to the condition that it shall not by way of trade or otherwise, be lent, resold, hired out or otherwise circulated, without the publisher's prior consent, in any form of binding or cover other than that in which it is published.

www.ukiyoto.com

Preface

Transgenderism is part of our biological evolution. Transgender people have existed in our world since ancient times. But they have often been marginalized and discriminated against.

The United Nations recognized the discrimination against and the importance of transgender rights. In 2011, the United Nations Human Rights Council passed a resolution calling for an end to discrimination based on sexual orientation and gender identity. It called on member states to take action to protect the rights of transgender people. This means it asked its member countries to frame laws to protect their rights.

Transgenders have been part of Indian society for centuries. In recent years, there has been a growing awareness of the issues faced by them. There have been efforts to promote their rights and improve their status in society. In *National Legal Services Authority v. Union of India Writ Petition (Civil) No. 400 of 2012* decided on 15 April 2014, the Supreme Court legally recognized transgenders as a third gender.

This was followed by the passing of the Transgender Persons (Protection of Rights) Act, 2019 and a host of measures criminalizing discrimination against transgenders and providing them a number of much needed benefits.

In this book, I have attempted to provide a brief history of transgenderism and information about the laws and rights of transgender people in India. I have provided detailed information how transgender people can obtain their certificate and identity cards (transgender card) and avail of the benefits due to them.

I have attached the two following Government pamphlets:

1. Application and Procedure for Scholarships.

2. Guidelines for Garima Greh or Shelter Homes for Transgenders. One major lacuna in the law is that since transgender is a separate (third) gender, and same gender marriages are not permissible in

India so far, I do not see how transgenders can marry amongst themselves.

Any transgender in India can apply for registration as transgender and issue of certificate and identity card through the following web site:

https://transgender.dosje.gov.in/Applicant/Registration/DisplayForm1

"The Portal provides the facility for transgender person to apply for certificate and identity card from across the country without physical interface through a seamless end to end mechanism. The Transgender certificate & identity card are nationally recognised and provided by the Ministry of Social Justice & Empowerment, the certificate is a mandatory document to avail the welfare measures being provided under the SMILE scheme.

The applicant can monitor, edit, track the status of their application through their login id ensuring transparency throughout the procedure. They are also provided with a grievance redressal mechanism wherein, the applicant can post their grievances pertaining to delay in the certification process which would be then forwarded to the concerned authority for resolution at the earliest. The portal acts as a facilitator between the districts authorities and beneficiaries for easy access to Transgender Certificate and Identity Cards as per their self-perceived identity which is an important provision of The Transgender Persons (Protection of Rights) Act, 2019 & Transgender Persons (Protection of Rights) Act 2020."

I feel this is a much needed book to help the transgenders. I am sure this will help them. Please let me know if you have any questions relating to transgenders.

email: eleena100@hotmail.com

Binoy Gupta

Contents

Back Ground	1
Rights of Transgender Persons and How To Obtain Them	7
Chapter III Recognition Of Identity Of Transgender Persons	8
Chapter II Prohibition Against Discrimination	9
Chapter IV Welfare Measures By Goverment	10
Chapter VII National Council For Trangender Persons	12
Chapter VIII Offences And Penalties	13
Chapter IX Miscellaneous	14
Male, Female, Transgenders and Change of Gender	15
Transgender Persons (Protection of Rights) Act, 2019	20
Transgender Persons (Protection of Rights) Rules, 2020	21
Application process to obtain Scholarships	22
Shelter Homes for Transgenders	23
About the Author	*24*

Back Ground

Transgenderism is part of our biological evolution. Transgender people have existed since ancient times. A wide range of societies had traditional third gender roles and accepted trans-people in some form. We do not know the precise history.

In India, we find mention of transgender people – hizras – in the Ramayana. But then they were despised. This issue reached the Supreme Court of India. It considered the matter in National Legal Services Authority v. Union of India Writ Petition (Civil) No.400 of 2012 decided on 15 April 2014 and held that transgender should be treated as the third gender. I am reproducing a few important paras from that Judgement:

"Lord Rama, in the epic Ramayana, was leaving for the forest upon being banished from the kingdom for 14 years, turns around to his followers and asks all the 'men and women' to return to the city. Among his followers, the hijras alone do not feel bound by this direction and decide to stay with him. Impressed with their devotion, Rama sanctions them the power to confer blessings on people on auspicious occasions like childbirth and marriage, and also at inaugural functions which, it is believed set the stage for the custom of badhai in which hijras sing, dance and confer blessings".

Para 13 of the S.C. order

The modern concept of being transgender, and gender in general, developed in the mid-1900s. The term transgender refers to a person whose gender identity is different from the sex assigned at birth. For example, a transgender person who was assigned female at birth may in later years identify as male, a combination of male and female, or neither. The term transgenderism was first used by the Psychiatrist John F. Oliven of Columbia University in his reference book Sexual Hygiene and Pathology in 1965.

From the 18th century onwards, with the onset of colonial rule, the situation in India changed drastically. The British enacted the Criminal Tribes Act, 1871 to supervise the deeds of Hijras/TG community which deemed the entire community of Hijras persons as innately 'criminal' and 'addicted to the systematic commission of non-bailable offences'. The Act provided for the registration, surveillance and control of certain criminal tribes and eunuchs and penalized eunuchs, who were registered, and appeared to be dressed or ornamented like a woman, in a public street or place, as well as those who danced or played music in a public place. Such persons could be arrested without warrant and sentenced to imprisonment up to two years or fine or both.

Unfortunately, throughout history, transgender people have been subjected to discrimination and violence. This is mainly due to a lack of understanding leading to non acceptance of people who do not conform to the traditional and accepted gender norms. Transphobia, or a negative attitude against the transgenders, is often rooted in ignorance, fear, and prejudice. However, not everyone despises transgender people. There have always been many people who have supported and advocated rights for transgenders.

The available data indicates that the percentage of people who identify as transgender tends to be roughly consistent around the world - ranging from 1-3%. On this basis, India must be having around 2.5 crore transgenders. There is a separate law for them giving them protections, government help and support. In the following chapter, I have tried to explain the legalities and formalities in simple words.

It is worth noting that the Karnataka Government has decided to provide one percent reservation in government jobs for the people of the transgender community. It is the first state in the country to do so.

United Nation Human Rights Commission

On 17 June 2011, the United Nations Human Rights Council passed its First-Ever Historic Resolution on Sexual Orientation and Gender Identity resolution on human rights violations based on sexual orientation and gender identity.

The resolution requested the High Commissioner for Human Rights to prepare a study on violence and discrimination on the basis of sexual orientation and gender identity, and called for a panel discussion by the Human Rights Council to discuss the findings of the study in a constructive and transparent manner, and to consider appropriate follow-up.

Pursuant to this resolution, the Commissioner for Human Rights submitted to the Human Rights Council a report documenting discriminatory laws and practices and acts of violence against individuals based on their sexual orientation and gender identity, and how international human rights law can be used to end violence and related human rights violations based on sexual orientation and gender identity.

Supreme Court of India

The matter went up to the Supreme Court of India. In National Legal Services Authority v. Union of India Writ Petition (Civil) No. 400 of 2012 decided on 15 April 2014, the Hon'ble Supreme Court went deep into the history, present problems and the practices pertaining to tansgenders in different countries. I am reproducing a few important portions from that decision.

2. We are, in this case, concerned with the grievances of the members of Transgender Community (for short 'TG community') who seek a legal declaration of their gender identity than the one assigned to them, male or female, at the time of birth and their prayer is that non-recognition of their gender identity violates Articles 14 and 21 of the Constitution of India. Hijras/Eunuchs, who also fall in that group, claim legal status as a third gender with all legal and constitutional protection.

Para 2 of the SC Judgement

12. TG Community comprises of Hijras, eunuchs, Kothis, Aravanis, Jogappas, Shiv-Shakthis etc. and they, as a group, have got a strong historical presence in our country in the Hindu mythology and other religious texts. The Concept of tritiya prakrti or napunsaka has also

been an integral part of vedic and puranic literatures. The word 'napunsaka' has been used to denote absence of procreative capability.

Para 12 of the SC Judgement

13. Lord Rama, in the epic Ramayana, was leaving for the forest upon being banished from the kingdom for 14 years, turns around to his followers and asks all the 'men and women' to return to the city. Among his followers, the hijras alone do not feel bound by this direction and decide to stay with him. Impressed with their devotion, Rama sanctions them the power to confer blessings on people on auspicious occasions like childbirth and marriage, and also at inaugural functions which, it is believed set the stage for the custom of badhai in which hijras sing, dance and confer blessings.

Para 13 of the SC Judgement

19. Gender identity is one of the most-fundamental aspects of life which refers to a person's intrinsic sense of being male, female or transgender or transsexual person. A person's sex is usually assigned at birth, but a relatively small group of persons may born with bodies which incorporate both or certain aspects of both male and female physiology. At times, genital anatomy problems may arise in certain persons, their innate perception of themselves, is not in conformity with the sex assigned to them at birth and may include pre and post-operative transsexual persons and also persons who do not choose to undergo or do not have access to operation and also include persons who cannot undergo successful operation. Countries, all over the world, including India, are grappled with the question of attribution of gender to persons who believe that they belong to the opposite sex.....

Para 19 of the SC Judgement

45. Transgender people, as a whole, face multiple forms of oppression in this country. Discrimination is so large and pronounced, especially in the field of health care, employment, education, leave aside social exclusion.....

Para 45 of the SC Judgement

49. Indian Law, on the whole, only recognizes the paradigm of binary genders of male and female, based on a person's sex assigned by birth, which permits gender system....

Para 49 of the SC Judgement

68. Recognition of one's gender identity lies at the heart of the fundamental right to dignity. Gender, as already indicated, constitutes the core of one's sense of being as well as an integral part of a person's identity. Legal recognition of gender identity is, therefore, part of right to dignity and freedom guaranteed under our Constitution.

Para 68 of the SC Judgement

106. For these reasons, we are of the opinion that even in the absence of any statutory regime in this country, a person has a constitutional right to get the recognition as male or female after SRS, which was not only his/her gender characteristic but has become his/her physical form as well. (2) Re: Right of TG to be identified and categorized as "third gender".

Para 106 of the SC Judgement

129. We, therefore, declare:

(1) Hijras, Eunuchs, apart from binary gender, be treated as "third gender" for the purpose of safeguarding their rights under Part III of our Constitution and the laws made by the Parliament and the State Legislature. &

(2) Transgender persons' right to decide their self-identified gender is also upheld and the Centre and State Governments are directed to grant legal recognition of their gender identity such as male, female or as third gender.

(3) We direct the Centre and the State Governments to take steps to treat them as socially and educationally backward classes of citizens and extend all kinds of reservation in cases of admission in educational institutions and for public appointments. *Para 129 of the SC Judgement*

An Expert Committee had already been constituted to make an in-depth study of the problems faced by the Transgender community and suggest remedial measures. The Supreme Court directed the Expert

Committee to examine the recommendations based on the legal declaration made in this Judgment and implement it within six months.

By order dated 22 October 2013, the Ministry of Social Justice and Empowerment constituted an Expert Committee to make an in-depth study of the problems being faced by the Transgender Community and suggest suitable measures to ameliorate their conditions. The Committee submitted its detailed report on 27 January 2014. This report led to the enactment of the

Transgender Persons (Protection of Rights) Act, 2019, Rules and various concessions and assistance given to the transgenders.

Rights of Transgender Persons and How To Obtain Them

The Transgender Persons (Protection of Rights) Act, 2019 was passed by the Parliament on 5 December 2019 and came into effect from 10 January 2020. The Act was enacted to provide protection of rights of transgender persons and their welfare and for matters connected therewith and incidental thereto. The Transgender Persons (Protection of Rights) Rules were framed in 2020. The Rules contain the different forms and the detailed procedures. In this chapter, I am giving an overview of the different provisions of the Act and Rules. The rights of the transgenders and how to obtain them.

Definition of Transgender Person

The Act has given a very wide and comprehensive definition

Section 2(k) "Transgender person" means a person whose gender does not match with the gender assigned to that person at birth and includes trans-man or trans-woman (whether or not such person has undergone Sex Reassignment Surgery or hormone therapy or laser therapy or such other therapy), person with intersex variations, genderqueer and person having such socio-cultural identities as kinner, hijra, aravani and jogta.

Section 2(k) of TG Act

Chapter III Recognition Of Identity Of Transgender Persons

4. Recognition of identity of transgender person.—

(1) A transgender person shall have a right to be recognised as such, in accordance with the provisions of this Act.

Note: The Government does not have any power to declare any person transgender. The concerned person has to apply for and obtain the transgender certificate called Certificate of Identity.

Chapter II Prohibition Against Discrimination

Section 3   No person or establishment shall discriminate against a transgender person on any of the grounds enumerated in Section 3(a) to 3(i).

Note: This Section prohibits discrimination against transgenders in the following areas - educational establishments; employment and occupation; healthcare services; use of public services; right of movement; immoveable property; contesting for and holding public office; unfair treatment in Government or private establishments.

Chapter IV Welfare Measures By Goverment

8. Obligation of appropriate Government.—(1) The appropriate Government shall take steps to secure full and effective participation of transgender persons and their inclusion in society.

Note|: This Section requires the Government to take welfare measures; formulate welfare schemes and programmes; take steps for the rescue, protection and rehabilitation of transgender persons and take appropriate measures to promote and protect their right to participate in cultural and recreational activities.

How to get a Transgender Certificate - called Certificate of Identity

5. Application for certificate of identity.—A transgender person may make an application to the District Magistrate for issuing a certificate of identity as a transgender person, in such form and manner, and accompanied with such documents, as may be prescribed: Provided that in the case of a minor child, such application shall be made by a parent or guardian of such child.

Note: A transgender person has to apply to the District Magistrate for issue of a transgender certificate in Form No. 1 of the TG Rules. This has to be accompanied with an Affidavit on Stamp Paper of Rs. 10 affirmed before a Notary Public in Form No. 2 of the TG Rules. The Government has no power to declare any one a transgender. It is the sole discretion of the applicant. No Medical certificate or examination is required.

6. Issue of certificate of identity.—

(1) The District Magistrate shall issue to the applicant a certificate of identity indicating the gender of such person as transgender.

(2) The gender of transgender person shall be recorded in all official documents in accordance with certificate issued under sub-section (1).

(3) A certificate issued to a person under sub-section (1) shall confer rights and be a proof of recognition of his identity as a transgender person.

Note: The District Magistrate has to issue the certificate in Form No. 3 of the TG Rules showing the applicant's gender as transgender. This is conclusive proof and shall be recorded in all official documents. The District Magistrate shall also issue an Transgender Identity Card in Form No. 5 & 6 of the TG Rules.

*It is mandatory for the district authorities to issue transgender certificates & ID cards within 30 days of Receiving the Application.

7. Change in gender.—

(1) If after the issue of a certificate of identify, a transgender person undergoes surgery to change gender either as a male or female, such person may make an application, along with a certificate issued to that effect by the Medical Superintendent or Chief Medical Officer of the medical institution in which that person has undergone surgery, to the District Magistrate for revised certificate. (2) The District Magistrate shall, on being satisfied with the correctness of such certificate, issue a certificate indicating change in gender.

(3) The person who has been issued a certificate of identity under section 6 or a revised certificate under sub-section (2) can change the first name in the birth certificate and all other official documents relating to the identity of such person:

Provided that such change in gender and the issue of revised certificate under sub-section (2) shall not affect the rights and entitlements of such person under this Act.

Note: A transgender person who undergoes surgery to change gender can apply to the District Magistrate for revised certificate in Form No. 1 of the TG Rules. The District Magistrate shall issue revised certificate of identity in Form No. 4 of the TG Rules.

Chapter VII National Council For Trangender Persons

16. National Council for Transgender Persons.—

(1) The Central Government shall constitute a National Council for Transgender Persons to exercise the powers and perform the functions assigned to it under this Act.

Note: The Sub-section 2 lists the persons who will be members of this Council.

17. Functions of Council.—The National Council shall perform the following functions:— (a) advise the Central Government on the formulation of policies, etc. (b) monitor and evaluate the impact of policies and programmes (c) review and coordinate the activities of all the departments of Government and other Governmental and non-Governmental Organisations dealing with matters relating to transgender persons; (d) redress the grievances of transgender persons.

Note: This Section lists the functions of the National Council.

Chapter VIII Offences And Penalties

18. Offences and penalties.— Whoever violates the provisions of this Act relating to the rights of the transgenders shall be punishable with imprisonment for a term which shall not be less than six months but which may extend to two years and with fine.

Note: This section prescribes the penalty for violation of the rights of transgenders - imprisonment from 6 months to 2 years and fine

Chapter IX Miscellaneous

19. Grants by Central Government.—The Central Government shall, from time to time credit such sums to the National Council as may be necessary for carrying out the purposes of this Act.

Note: The Central Government shall, from time to time, give money to the National Council to carry out the purposes of this Act.

22. Power of appropriate Government to make rules.—

(1) The appropriate Government may, make rules for carrying out the provisions of this Act.

Note: This Provision empowers every state government to make its own rules including prescribing its own Forms for various purposes.

Male, Female, Transgenders and Change of Gender

Sex and Gender are totally different concepts. Sex is typically determined at birth by examining the external genitals. Males usually have a penis and scrotum. Females have a vagina and vulva. This is the classification normally given in the birth certificate and in the hospital and municipal records.

Gender refers to the social and cultural roles, behaviors, expressions, and identities of men, women, or gender-diverse people. It is a complex interplay of psychology, society, and culture rather than just biological sex.

Sex – Male or Female

From a biological point, sex is categorized as either male or female based on reproductive anatomy, chromosomes and hormone levels.

Those with XX chromosomes are categorized as female and XY as male. However, variants like XXY or XO exist. Genetic testing alone does not always align with physical sex characteristics or gender identity. Some individuals with XY chromosomes have female external anatomy due to conditions like androgen insensitivity syndrome.

Sex determination can be quite complex in some cases of intersex conditions.

Medical Tests for determining Biological Sex

There are no definitive medical tests that can conclusively prove whether a person is male, female or transgender. Some of the medical tests and assessments commonly used are:

- Karyotyping: Analyzing chromosomes can show whether someone has XX (typically female) or XY (typically male) pairs. It can identify variations like XXY in Klinefelter syndrome.

- Hormone levels: Measuring testosterone, estrogen, LH, FSH levels provides clues about gonadal sex. Testosterone dominance suggests male sex, while estrogen dominance suggests female sex.

- Imaging studies: Ultrasounds, CT scans or MRIs of reproductive organs help identify the presence of ovaries, uterus, vagina (female sex) or testes, penis, prostate (male sex). However, as intersex conditions demonstrate, there is natural variation in genital development. Some individuals have ambiguous genitalia not clearly definable as male or female.

Genetic testing: Testing for SRY gene or other sex-related genes provides information about genetic sex.

Gender Identity

Gender identity refers to a person's internal sense of being male, female, both or neither. It may or may not correspond with the sex assigned at birth. Medical tests are not very useful for determining gender identity

Tests for determining Gender Identity:

- Clinical evaluation: A mental health professional can diagnose gender dysphoria based on psychiatric criteria like discomfort with anatomical sex, desire for opposite gender roles etc.

- Hormone levels: Measuring hormones may offer clues but can't give definitive proof about gender identity. Hormone testing can measure levels of androgens like testosterone versus estrogens. But hormone levels vary greatly across individuals and populations, so there are no clear cut-off levels that would definitively categorize someone as male or female. For example, some women have higher testosterone while some men have lower levels.

- Brain scans: Studies show transgender individuals may have certain structural and functional brain patterns similar to their gender identity, but these are not conclusive.

Transgenders

The age old binary male-female sex classification fails to capture the intricate variation in human sexual development. Gender further complicates the picture, as a person's identity may differ from biological attributes. Transgender individuals may have a gender identity different from the sex assigned at birth. Non-binary people identify outside of male-female categories.

Transgender has been legally recognized as the third Gender. Defining and differentiating between male, female and transgender individuals involves complex biological, social, and legal considerations. Medical testing alone cannot capture the full complexity of human sex and gender.

For transgenders and gender diverse people, medical interventions like hormone therapy and surgeries help better align physical sex characteristics with gender identity. However, procedures are not universally accessible or desired. Individuals ultimately have to define their own gender based on a deeply felt, internal sense of self.

While the above tests may provide supporting evidence, they cannot offer 100% conclusive proof of whether someone is male, female or transgender. Comprehensive psychological, medical and social evaluation is needed for determining gender identity. Mental health professionals can help by making a diagnosis of gender dysphoria based on clinical assessment criteria.

Gender Change - Sex Reassignment Surgery (SES)

A few persons are not happy with their gender. They may have:

- A strong conviction of being or wish to become the opposite gender.
- A persistent dislike or discomfort with their sexual anatomy.

- A strong desire to obtain the physical features of the opposite gender.

- A strong preference for the clothing, activities and roles associated with the opposite gender.

Section 15 of the Transgender Persons (Protection of Rights) Act, 2019, reproduced hereunder, has recognized this and permits such persons to under go sex reassignment surgery (SES) and hormonal therapy:

"15. Healthcare facilities.—The appropriate Government shall take the following measures in relation to transgender persons, namely:—

(a) to set up separate human immunodeficiency virus Sero-surveillance Centres to conduct sero- surveillance for such persons in accordance with the guidelines issued by the National AIDS Control Organization in this behalf;

(b) to provide for medical care facility including sex reassignment surgery and hormonal therapy;

(c) before and after sex reassignment surgery and hormonal therapy counselling; (d) bring out a Health Manual related to sex reassignment surgery in accordance with the World Profession Association for Transgender Health guidelines;

(e) review of medical curriculum and research for doctors to address their specific health issues;

(f) to facilitate access to transgender persons in hospitals and other healthcare institutions and centres;

(g) provision for coverage of medical expenses by a comprehensive insurance scheme for Sex Reassignment Surgery, hormonal therapy, laser therapy or any other health issues of transgender persons.

If a person undergoes sex reassignment surgery to align their anatomy with their gender identity, they are legally and clinically classified according to their post-surgical sex. However, gender diverse people who transition, but do not opt for surgery, can also change their identity. Self-identification is paramount.

Sex change – Sex Reassignment Surgery (SRS) - decisions on

Chinder Pal Singh a female gender wanted to undergo SRS to get her gender identity changed from female to male for certain gender identity disorder. In this case, the Rajasthan High Court granted her permission for the purpose of sex reassignment surgery taking into consideration the provisions contained in the Central Act.

Chinder Pal Singh v. The Chief Secretary, Government of Rajasthan and others (S.B. Civil Writ Petition No. 14044 of 2021 decided on 25.5.2023) Rajasthan High Court.

Myra Grace Bandikalla (formerly known as Mr. Swaroop Rajarao Bandikalla), a transgenders' application for the purpose of facilitating her visit to Bangkok for getting SRS done was granted by the Bombay High Court. In this case, the petitioner was suffering from gender dysphoria and was accordingly desirous of SRS.

Mr. Swaroop Rajarao Bandikalla) v. Airport Authority of India and Others (Writ Petition (L) No. 1976 of 2018) order dated 4th July, 2018 of Bombay High Court.

Neha Singh, a woman constable in U.P. Police, an unmarried women found in herself all the traits of a male personality. She claimed she was suffering from Gender Dysphoria and wanted to undergo Sex Reassignment Surgery (SRS) to get herself identified and personalized as a male with true male physical character. She applied for necessary permission which was delayed. On 18.8.2023, the Allahabad High Court directed the Director General of Police to dispose off her application by 21.9. 2023.

Neha Singh Petitioner vs State Of U.P. And 2 Others WRIT - A No. - 7796 of 2023 – Allahabad High Court (matter pending)

Transgender Persons (Protection of Rights) Act, 2019

(It is in PDF Format marked Ch 5 – Insert)

Transgender Persons (Protection of Rights) Rules, 2020

(It is in PDF Format marked Ch 6 – Insert)

Application process to obtain Scholarships

(Scholarship Manual for Transgenders)

(It is in PDF Format marked Ch 7 – Insert)

Shelter Homes for Transgenders
(Guides lines for Garima Grehs)

(It is in PDF Format marked Ch 8 – Insert)

About the Author

Dr Binoy Gupta

Dr. Binoy Gupta is retired as a top bureaucrat in the Government of India. He holds a Ph.D. in law as well as a large number of post graduate degrees and diplomas. He has authored several books and written hundreds of articles. He believes this book is a must for transgenders.